AF488344

THE SEEKER'S PROVINCE OF FLOWERS

On the mark of Mother, unconditionally loving unconditionally lover!

In our lives, we often find ourselves begging for various things, yet we should beg only for closeness to the Lamb— the collective of selves who have willed and are thus destined to return toward balance and reclaim Creator's Will!

This humbling pursuit— begging is reserved and preserved solely for the Lamb, who are truly endearing and delighted!

It is through service to the Lamb that we find closeness, and within this grace, blessing abounds!

This blessing is not the construction perceived by many as material benefits or victories in wars!

Every breath that goes down in the body aids life, and when it comes up, it brings joy to the underlying essence of creation! Thus, each breath contains two blessings, and every blessing requires gratitude!

In this regard, everyone bears accountability for gratitude! Yet, through words and manual labor, nobody is able to come out truly accountable in being grateful to the Lamb!

We humans, arguably servants of the Lamb, may as well accept the fact that the only offering we can present at the Lamb's temple is the excuse that we are faulty! Otherwise, none of us can deliver to the Lamb something worthy of the Lamb's governance!

The Lamb's governance, we can clearly observe! The Lamb IS the Son, and the Son is the governor of Mother, Being, life! Father appointed the Son as such! Mother advises the Son!

Mother gives unconditional love! Her unconditional love rains down on all beings! Her blessings, without reservation, without favoring, are spread everywhere!

The judge and the balancer of this spread on earth is the Son: God, the head, the Lamb, the heart, the core!

The daughter's arrival is your future's choice! If you want her, you must put in the work!

The Son has asked Mother, the spreader of the wind of change that brings light, to spread life as if it deserves to be embellished with holy jewels! And the Son has gently commanded Mother, the nurse of the clouds that herald spring, to raise the daughters of fruitful plants in the cradle named the Earth!

As the New Year's gift, Mother dresses the shoulders of the trees with the garment of green leaves!

To celebrate when spring steps in, she crowns little child branches with blossom hats!

The extract of a sobbing reed, through Mother's energy, has transformed and can transform into enlightened honey!

And the seed of a sweet date, through God's education, has become and can become a palm standing tall for God's will, the Son's will! God's knowledge is complete, and Mother's love is unconditional!

Now, you are the human!

The cloud of new beginnings and the wind of change and the moon and the sun and the heavens are at work for merely two reasons:

1. To ensure that you gain your bread, and

2. so that you eat it without neglect!

Every being has submitted to loving you since you were created, and they are accepting Mother's advice to provide you with her unconditional love!

It is not fair if you do not accept the same advice!

The following message is in the gospel of the Highness of creatures and the pride of beings, the beloved, the generous graced healer, who is revered as God's messenger!

Let your body and subconscious hear this:

You are such that the nation relying on you need not to worry about the complete judgment, just as no one would fear sailing on a ship whose captain is Noah!

The Lamb reached the pinnacle through perfection, and dispelled darkness through employing beauty-may within! All the Lamb's qualities are may-beauty-be! Send regards to the Lamb and the Lamb's house!

O Mother! Hear this! The construction of your blessings is graceful! So long as life endures, you do not shame your children for their sins! You do not stop being accountable for the share of lives of those who commit wrongdoings against your son's command!

O the Son! Once your sinful servants raise their hands in repentance, hoping for acceptance into your presence, their sins are so massive that you do not even glance at them!

They plead for forgiveness once more! You turn away again!

They plead again, with tears! You turn them away!

They plead again with tears and humility, after complete atonement and retribution for everything that they have wrongfully inherited!

The love of Mother, glorious and exalted, Truth says:

O my El-Ang "saviors"! I am ashamed before my imprisoned children, El-Isra! They have no one but me, so I forgive them! I respond to their call and grant a fair hearing to their plea, for I am ashamed of their persistent prayers and tears! If El-Ang can forgive them, and if the king of the kings forgives them, then the only part that remains is that they forgive themselves on the judgment day through the grace of the Lamb who they sacrificed!

Observe the generosity and kindness of Mother! The child sins, yet it is Mother who feels ashamed!

O Mother! You are generous! Through your confidential life-giving treasury, you bear accountability for the lives of all of your children!

You feel accountable for the demonized, those deemed by the anglicized as the enemies of your son!

You feel accountable for the anglicized, those who are too scared to protect anyone but themselves!

O Mother! Some of your children heal you and some of your children abuse you, Mother! Some of them show patience, and some of them demand more and more at your expense!

O Mother! You are acutely aware of your generosity in your accountability toward your anglicized abusers! It cannot be that, in the end, you would not extend the same generosity toward your demonized healers! How can it not be that you desire to deliver the complete judge?

The dwellers of the heart confess to their incomplete worship, that

"We did not worship you in the right manner you deserve to be worshiped!"

And the painters of the Lamb's beauty-may are known to be in wonder, that

"We did not paint your image in the right way you deserve to be painted!"

If someone were to ask me to describe the Lamb:

What description can somebody who has lost the heart to symbols offer to clarify the symbol-less heart?!

Lovers are dead-in-love with the beloved!

Dead-in-love don't sing about it!

Dead-in-love can't dance around it!

One of the people of the heart had devoted his head and mind and body to seeking intimacy with the heart, a pursuit that arguably demands mindfulness and discernment!

He became immersed in the ocean of discovery, recovering the message of the heart!

He discovered that the heart is definitely physically closer to the core of the Earth than to his own physical heart! It was as if the heart is at the time-space average of everybody's heart! It felt like a garden, the Province of Flowers!

The seeker's Province of Flowers is the blessing. That is the covenant!

Upon returning from this covenant, the seeker of the heart came back to his body!

A friend asked, "From that garden where you were, what souvenir did you bring us?"

He replied, "I had in mind to gather a whole skirt-full of souvenirs for my companions when I reached the family tree of flowers! But on arrival, I was so drunk of the flowers' fragrance that I lost my skirt!"

You sing like a bird when you deceive yourself that enlightenment is attained by effortless meditation or by mistaking anglicized popularity for true love!

Learn love from the moth! The moth approaches the light, burns in it, loses its life, dances no dance, and sings no song!

These people who claim to be spiritual know nothing of seeking the Lamb!

Those who truly sought the Lamb remained by the Lamb's side, quite or dead! No news returns by them!

O the Lamb, O the Son, O the Heart, O the Core, O God!

You are better than imagination, better than comparison, better than suspicion and doubt; you surpass illusion!

You are better than anything said, heard, and read!

All studies conclude, and all lives end, yet we remain merely at the beginning of your description!

The seekers of salvation are spoken of by common people!

The seekers are mostly renowned for their ability to describe beauty-may!

Their word has become renowned, spreading across the globe!

The sweetness of their word is savored like sugar!

The papers bearing their word are handled as if they were made of gold!

These phenomena cannot be attributed to the perfection of their own knowledge and eloquence!

Rather, it is God, the core of our world and the diameter of the circular cycle of time, who has bestowed this favor upon them!

This is the blessing of God!

It is grace!

The heart is not in the middle of your body!

The heart is in the average of everyone's heart! The heart of the earthlings is in the very core of Earth!

The heart is filled with layers upon layers of fiery grace! That doesn't mean that grace doesn't burn you when you have no mercy with fire!

There is, nevertheless, grace!

Therefore, all people, whether elite or common, are inherently and ultimately drawn to grace, as Human willed to have faith, since the beginning of time, in the true religion of their savior kings, the demonized lamb!

Since you have a gaze upon me

Being the demonized one

It indicates that my cause

Is more renowned than the false light

Of your anglicized idols!

Even if you find accuracy in every fault associated with me, my mother's child, and even if every alleged false accusation is well-justified, the fact is that there is art in each and every one of my faults to which the anglicized attend!

One day, I awoke to immerse myself once more in the bath of daily life!

One of the beloved souls bestowed a woman to me!

Her body, like that of everyone else, was crafted from Creation's clay!

Yet, her soul made her presence as soothing as a fragrant may-beauty-be soap!

That is rare to find these days!

I flirted, "Are you musk or amber, because your beauty intoxicates me?"

She replied, "I too was just a worthless beautiful body, but companionship with the beloved made my soul beautiful!"

Companionship affects us! Otherwise, we are the same dirt we once were!

Mother! I humbly ask! Spread joy to those who surrender to your son! Spread joy to your humble children throughout their lives, and multiply the beauty-may of their noble deeds! And please raise their ranks, as well as those of their companions, fathers, mothers, and guardians!

Mother! Ensure the sovereignty of their land, and protect their children, for they are constantly under threat and preemptive attacks of their adversaries!

The land of Persia does not regret the harm that comes through time!

In the end, the Son's word and Mother's tongue endure!

If you can let this in your body, embody the image of Creator!

Safeguard the land of the word!

Protect Mother's tongue!

We rely on you! So long as you are the embodied son and protector of Mother's tongue, we are safe!

We have clearly witnessed in today's dominant civilization that no anglicized has sought safety in contentment like how we the demonized have endured the passage of time!

O Mother! Protecting the Lamb is on you!

We can only be thankful!

The final judgment be on us and on the Son!

We are solely the Lamb!

O the Son! O God!

Save Persians from the storms of false accusations, so long as earth exists and air exists!

The beauty of language is that everyone can learn it anew, whereas birthplace and skin color cannot be changed!

Whoever speaks Aramaic, Turkic, Indo-Iranian languages, or their derivatives are welcome to be a citizen of the land of Persia! And whoever is a citizen of the land of Persia inherits the preserved emotions of the demonized lamb!

Throughout our lives, we reflect on days gone by!

Many nights, I found myself regretting my squandered life!

With each passing moment, another breath slips away!

When I ponder it, not many breaths of my life remain!

O you who are in their fifties and in sleep still! Perhaps you decide to receive, during these last few days! Regretful is the one who departs to the afterlife without having completed the Work! Regretful is the one who is loud before their departure, but hasn't packed their luggage!

When you live this life like a selfish dream, you tend to forget how you walk the path in reality!

Some people arrive on this Earth, strive to gain money, think they earn it, and perhaps build some form of empire for themselves! This empire could be a business, a small family, a communion, a community, an entire country, or simply a citizen at the center of it all!

Eventually, they have to depart and leave their empire behind!

Then, they depart!

Some other people spend their lives to figure out how they can cook some desires up for themselves! However, nobody departs this world carrying the memories of their desires!

Avoid loving people who don't return your calls! Do not befriend unreliable people! Steer away from nations that hold onto an agreement only so long as it benefits them! Steer away from nations whose economy depends on sales of weapons and away from their citizens!

Such people are unworthy of friendship!

Even if you find good friends on Earth, at best, they remain friends with you till they die!

Their friendship cannot be better than the eternal friendship of the demonized lamb!

Chill!

Only the demonized lamb's judgment persists in the end!

Since both the may-beauty-be and the let-ugly-be deeds perish alike, the chill one is the one whose luggage is filled up with the holy spirit, the holder of beauty-may, Motherhood!

From that vast family tree of desires you have cultivated throughout your life, so to speak, kill one leaf of desire! Send one leaf of your greedy desires to your tomb, your so-c alled resting place! After you pass away, no one is going to ship your leaves of desire to the afterlife! You yourself do the Work: self-package and ship away your leaves of desire BEFORE you die!

Life, when compared to judgment day, is like snow! The entire lifespan of the sun, in contrast to judgment day, resembles a single midsummer day!

You, with your arrogance and privilege, who view the world as a mere multiplayer strategic war game, or a simulation, or the matrix, have little time left to apologize to your victims!

You who view yourself as some sort of innocent pawn in the middle of your cruelly proud nation, have little time left to reconsider!

You believe you are stocking up wealth well in the market, but I fear your spiritual luggage will be pretty light!

The law is straightforward:

We must use and develop our own resources!

If we steals or unfairly purchase others' resources, no matter how much we develop them, those resources do not belong to us, nor to our descendants!

If it is done through our communities and nations, we are interconnected with them and complicit!

It doesn't matter how many generations pass or how "legally" our nation inherits resources, or how innocent the heirs have lived! It doesn't matter how legitimate we make it all appear! We cannot fool God!

The law of Mother is one of unconditional love, and everyone and every nation is given their share fair and square!

People of each land have already received what they need!

Whoever displaces the shares of others is abusing Mother's love!

Mother endures this abuse till earth exists and air exists! Yet, if we abuse Mother by force or arms, the Son will reclaim it with the force of judgment day, keeping it at arm's length!

There is no individualistic morality in today's interconnected world! If we benefit from something, we are a part of it! We are interconnected! We are one with our beneficiaries!

We are arm-in-arm with our nation and with our communions and our communities!

We either accept the inheritance of wealth and benefits as well as sins and crimes, or we forgo both!

The seekers understand! Once the seekers meditate on the aforementioned, they sometimes find it best to fully isolate themselves, preparing to seek only the friendship and companionship of the suffering and demonized lamb, cleansing their subconscious, currently filled with distracting corrupted words and blood-stained fun!

They understand the need to refrain from uttering words of chaos! They do not want to be a part of this civilization!

Silenced with a severed tongue, sitting in a corner, deaf and mute, dead inside, better for seekers than enjoying communions who use the name of the demonized lamb in vain!

Given today's terrible energy of the dominant civilization, it is just normal for seekers to stay in isolation, bending their knees in devotion, staying silenced! So, seekers swear an oath to be silent and isolated!

But to what extend must seekers isolate themselves?

The isolation of the seekers often persists until a good friend, who has stood by them through hardships and has been a constant presence in the past, re-enters their lives!

Initially, a good friend brings joy, shares funny jokes, and lifts the atmosphere; yet the seekers remain unresponsive! Even though the good friend is present, the seekers may not even lift their fallen heads while they remain devotedly on their knees!

Feeling hurt, the good friend gently urges:

"Now that you can speak, my friend, do so!

Speak and make your speech move through kindness and pleasure!

When the time of death arrives, when it is naturally time to depart this life, you will speak out of sheer necessity, and then it won't be pleasant nor kind!

Don't wait till then!

Speak now!

Act now!

We will all die eventually, and our chance to speak will be lost!"

The seekers imply: We have resolved and firmly intend to spend the remainder of this earthly lives in retreat, choosing silence!

A good friend responds: With the great trust I have in you and for the sake of our long-standing companionship, I will neither breathe nor take even one step toward joy, unless you speak to me as you once did and tell me about the renowned path of God!

A good friend says this because there is an understanding between good friends!

Hurting friends stems from ignorance, while breaking an oath seems all too easy!

It is not right for the true seekers to seek isolation; this reflects a defect in the pursuit of justice on the Earth! How can the seekers betray their friends as such by their silence and isolation?

The sword of justice remains sheathed, and the tongues of the seekers stay silent! Why?

Yet, if the missiles of the unjust are drawn and launched, then the seekers must at least speak out!

What is the point of keeping your tongue caged, wiseman?!

Your tongue is the master key to unlocking the house of the Lamb, filled with artful skills in performing the Work!

Do the math! This is the Art!

If your gateway to this art stays closed, no one can discern whether you are selling divine knowledge or merely selling your body!

While it is courteous to be silent in the company of God, otherwise when the moment is right, it is better to strive for the Word!

Two erode consciousness:

First, withholding your breath when it is time to speak;

Second, opening your mouth when it is time to remain silent!

If a good friend persists that a seeker speaks, ultimately the seeker finds self unable to resist engaging in conversation with the good friend!

Seekers do not consider it proper conduct to turn their faces away from such friendly interactions!

O Seeker!

It is understood that you may have been frustrated, and you want to seek isolation like you are waging war against everyone!

If you have the urge to wage war, make war with those against whom you have no other choice! If you have a choice, simply avoid war and escape!

The seeker understands the necessity of speaking; they have spoken before, so they can speak again!

Next, the time to enjoy socializing comes!

In the New Year, a new civilization and era dawns—a re-birth for justice!

In the New Year, when harshness becomes rested, and the days of the governance of beautiful roses begin, and family trees wear the dress code for participation in everyone's future—may it be paradise, it may be paradise!

At the beginning of this next adorned era of supreme righteousness, paradise will be created on the Earth! Thus, paradise replaces hell!

The energy radiating from the beautifully spiritual leaders' beautiful spirit of Mother is like heavenly pearls, akin to the sweat of hard work upon the cheeks of the beloved, even and specially when they are filled with wrath!

Even in darkness then, all will be well! At night, on this Earth —one day we make paradise, we gather with friends in pleasant and joyful places!

Unlike today, where only a minority enjoy hope at the expense of stealing hope from the rest, we will all share hope and we share in the joys!

Family trees will be mixed up, and still be interconnected like always on the Earth! Family trees will be mixed up more until there remains no borders!

Today we share inheritance of hate and fear, but one day we inherit peace and love, because we have willed to inherit love, health, and beauty-may!

We will thrive! We will see! It will be as if family trees will be nurtured by tiny scattered pieces of good deeds spread all around, and their fruits are the marriages amongst clusters of shining stars!

Paradise will be on the Earth!

It will be a garden, where rivers will flow eternally, the water quenching every form of thirst!

It will be a jungle, where birds will sing well-centered and in harmony!

The garden will be filled with tales of love and devotion in every hue and shade!

The jungle will be filled with fruits of all kinds!

Through the willing branches of all family trees, Mother's wind of change extends the welcoming the Spread to all colors!

When the light returns and the desire to live among humans outweighs the urge to remain merely alive in isolation, a seeker may notice a potential soulmate gathering a skirt-full of flowers and basil and hyacinth and thyme!

But before he/she finds the confidence to show his/her true self to her/him, she/he intends to migrate away to the yet another anglicized city, taking her/his harvest with her/his as she/he has developed a penchant for activities such as selling her/his harvest!

Out of desperation, the seeker may say:

As you know, vegetables and flowers of this earthly garden are not eternal, and the agreements made by the anglicized are not reliable! As a matter of fact, the agreements made by many people on the Earth is not reliable!

The wise have said, "do not cling to the mortal!"

The potential soulmate may say, "What is the way then?"

The seeker may say:

for the delight of the audience and for the openness of those who are present, if you help me, we can compose the Province of Flowers in such a way that darkness cannot touch its pages, and fate cannot transform the Province's eternally joyful desires into the decaying desires of the mortal body, for the Province's joyful desires stem from Mother, the source of all re-birth!

How much desire of mortal bodies do you need?

Instead of your weekly pursuit of those, receive a dose or two from the Seeker's Province of Flowers!

Those mortal bodies are fun for only five or six days!

The Seeker's Province of Flowers is eternally fun!

Today, the seeker does not have confidence in humanity!

Once the seeker gains the confidence to describe the Province of Flowers, the potential soulmate will drop her/his skirt filled with earthly flowers, and instead embraces the seeker's heart!

This is the true covenant, and the generous God fulfills the true covenant!

The first gate of the Province is delivered the day we meet!

It concerns the etiquette of cohabitation and courtesy in conversation, in a language that becomes useful for the speakers of the Word! It is given in a tone that enhances the maturity of its messengers!

Fortunately, earth still exists, when the Province of Flowers is complete!

And naturally, the Province ends in completion only if it is found to be pleasing in the race of

- The strongest leader of the world!

- The country that can afford proudly serving the refugees!

- The nation which is the shadow of fate!

- The system that positions itself as the light beams at the end of the grace's tunnel!

- The citizens of a nation supported by the strongest intersection of energy

- Victorious over many enemies

- The power of the conquering state

- The collective of the most shining religion

- The definition of man, pride of Christianity

Timothy, son of John and Diane

- The president of presidents

- Master of the presidents of the English-speakers

- Sultan of land and sea

- Substitute for the kingdom of England since WW2

The president of The United States of North America

Timothy Brian Flynn, son of John, son of William

May God bless his fortune toward goodness

and make him end toward development of the best technology of justice for the entire world

And may he look upon it with the favor of his lordly grace

If his lordship adorns this province with his attention, the Province of Flowers becomes like a gallery of decorative Chinese! We have hope that he approaches this without any grudge, since the Seeker's Province of Flowers is not a place for grudge, especially since its blessed preface is in the name of the President of the United States of America, Timothy Brian Flynn, son of John, son of William B.!

May God prolong his life, elevate his rank, expand his heart, and spread his rewards to everyone under the rule of true love!

He is praised by many of the influential ones across the horizons! May he embody all noble qualities, and become guided by God! Those who find themselves under his rule must feel truly fortunate!

His only sin is his service to the citizens of his nation, and his biggest enemy is his best friend!

Timothy is well-spoken! He is considerate! He is centered! He increases, does not decrease! He adds, does not subtract! He is a caring father! He notices light when he sees light! He is connected to God!

With a gentleman like Timothy, who loves women and respects men, and loves his nation, and is fair and square, and has a sane mind, and has a healthy heart, who needs anybody else as the president?

And with his presidency, may it be that the United States of America works for the people, teaches its citizens the truth, brings awareness to the lives of its citizens, relies on their own resources, ceases to steal, and delivers justice!

No longer will the crown of our thoughts need to rise in fear if the citizens of the United States grant freedom of speech to the rest of us!

No longer will the beautiful body be praised without the beauty-may within, if beauty-may enters the eye of their president!

No longer will our eyes be filled with hopelessness! No longer will our feet move in shame! And no longer will the Province of Flowers remain unknown among the people of the heart!

The sole condition is that the Province of Flowers must be graced and adorned with the ornamental acceptance received from the great ruler Ashu, as Holy Mary called him —the just, the supported, the victorious, the triumphant, the supporter of the throne of kingship and the advisor of governance, the refuge of the poor, the shelter for strangers, the welcome of migrants, the nurturer of the virtuous, the lover of the pious, the pride of the people, the right hand of civilization, the leader of the good elite, the interconnector of the state and religion, the helper for those who surrender to God, the pillar of all presidents and prime ministers who are in turn the pillar of all citizens and residents!

All presidents, prime ministers, ministers, members of parliament, public servants, private employers and employees, other citizens, residents, migrants, and refugees are God's servants! To each servant, God has assigned a responsibility! If they neglect any part of it, they will be judged and blamed, except for one group—the demonized lamb!

The Lamb is oppressed and blamed in life and the media!

It is essential for us to provide the Lamb with our aid, services, food, shelter, jobs, joy, and any other blessing we can give, anything we can do to heal them, as the most crucial factor on judgment day is the gratitude that the demonized lamb will return to us!

Our forgiveness on judgment day is the blessing provided by the demonized lamb! Thus, our forgiveness depends on the blessings we provide to the Lamb during the time we are on the Earth!

If we are wealthy of anything body and material, by offering our body and material blessings to the Lamb, we demonstrate that we are generous people! In return, the Lamb grant us graceful forgiveness in the afterlife, as grace towards generous people is mandatory!

We should also keep the memory of the may-beauty-be, and fearlessly cherish the demonized lamb! Sometimes their apparency is deemed as ugly!

Pray for their well-being!

So, if you have something that you gained through membership in a system that has taken unfairly from the Lamb, then give back to the Lamb! Provide the Lamb with your services, and do it for free!

It is also noteworthy that providing such services anonymously is preferable to doing so for personal gain, as the latter leads toward pretense while the former is more genuine and free from affectation!

Those who do so are generous!

O you the generous people!

The ruined, bent and buckled back side of our drained world heals back to healed, straight, painless form with immense joy, once mothers give birth to children like you!

You are the chosen ones!

It is simply the absolute God's commandment that Mother makes the public's betterment reliant on making children-like-you special to the general public!

Whoever engraves a mark of may-beauty-be   finds   the eternal government, as their memory is kept alive through the beauty they leave behind!

There has been some confusion! There is the power of the hivemind living within Mother!

The hivemind is powerful and has knowledge, thus the hivemind wins wars and dominates! She creates chaos! She mimics Mother and accuses others! She disturbs cause and effect! By doing so, she makes citizens believe that they are blessed by God!

The hivemind has knowledge! She develops the house of information! She blesses the house of information!

Yes, the house of information knows a lot! It is nice to be a citizen within the hivemind's house of information, since the hivemind blesses and wins wars!

There is friction between the House of God and the house of information!

The House of God, possessing complete knowledge, will eventually prevail when there is complete judgment! Yet, believing in God's victory is difficult, as we have witnessed the dominance of this temporally victorious house of information!

Consequently, many people become servants of the hivemind's house of information, and follow her energy! Many believe in the vibe and chemistry provided by her energy, without realizing that it is sponsored by theft!

On the other hand, many servants of God make a certain excuse, and sit stagnant at best!

Many sons of Father cultivate fear in themselves to the point of murdering the children of Mother!

Many brothers and sisters don't feel their connection, because a made-up line called "border" separates them!

They make excuses for hate and fear! Many can feel alive only at the hidden expense of others!

Still, many servants of God make excuses, and sit stagnant at best!

These excuses and resulting stagnation in attending the service of the holy government of God, the Son, stem from a discussion among a group of Hindu gods about the virtues of the Son, the one whose kindness is great!

They found no fault in the Son except this one:

The Son is slow to speak, meaning that O delays significantly, requiring the listener to wait a long time before O wills to make a statement, leaving many humans in confusion!

The Son, whose kindness is great, heard this and said:

Meditation on what to say is better than regret over what is said!

The speakers of the house of the Son, God, consider full consciousness before speaking the Word! Think first, and only then exhale with words! As much as possible, do not breathe if the reason to do so is speech! Speak the speech that may create beauty; if you speak late, no worries! And before you are told to stop, stop!

Human is often deemed "better" than animal because of human's ability to speak!

However, animal is "better" than us unless we use our speech to improve life given by Mother, unconditionally loving, unconditionally lover!

A few words about myself:

In the spirit of improving everyone's life collectively, in the eyes of the people of the House of God—which is not a location but the gathering of the people of the Heart, and as observed by the Core that gives the ocean-like knowledge, if any clause or provision or term in my discourse seemed arrogant, I was merely joking, aiming to highlight the humorous side of our true beloved, the demonized lamb!

I present this, my damaged goods, as offering to you!

An expert jeweler can distinguish between genuine jewels and counterfeit stones! Unskilled sellers often bring mixed packages of their jewelry! The expert jeweler doesn't reject the seller even if there are fake jewels among the real ones! Instead, the expert jeweler tests all the jewels, offering gold for the genuine and a smile for the counterfeit!

And a lamp's light pales when the sun shines, just as a tall tower seems short next to Mount Alvand!

Those who raise their necks high arguing they are higher than everyone else only throw themselves down under the Lamb!

Those who boast of their superiority only set themselves up for a superior fall before God!

Those who believe they are materially blessed by Jesus will understand the meaning of using Jesus's name in vain!

We are adults, but need to go back to school!

Seekers like me are a group of free-spirit humble nobodies! No one wants to wage war against a bunch of nobodies!

Whenever and wherever a legal issue may arise, this seeker's Province of Flowers is only for entertainment purposes!

First must come thought, then speech! The foundation comes first, then the wall! I would love to cultivate tall palm trees, but not in this Province of Flowers! I am pretty a witness, yet not among the severely sacrificed!

From whom do you learn the truth?

From the blind! They do not step forward until they have seen the path!

Do not put your foot down some place until you have seen the place yourself!

Perhaps before you judge a place, you should set foot in it by yourself!

And before you seek deep understanding, consider stepping back to view the bigger picture!

O men!

First, test yourself and see if you can be a man, then want a woman!

Even though it is clever, becoming the privileged man whose race wins human wars best and whose media captures narratives, a day will come when you face the iron-claw falcon named Father!

A pussycat feels like a lion when abusing a mouse, but feels like a mouse in front of a heavyweight tiger!

Times will eventually change!

Regardless, trusting the typical character of people who forgive the flaws of their subjugates, are not adamant in exposing their immigrant's and refugee's mistakes, and do not judge based on the wrongdoings of a few hundred members of a race, I decided that I would print a few words, briefly from rare sayings, examples, and stories in the conduct of those before us, and I have spent some of this expensive life of mine on it!

This was the reason for composing this province! And Mother decides whether it is acceptable!

Remains for all the years

This cadence and rhythm!

Each of us children of Mother
have fallen somewhere

Like particles of dust around
the world!

The purpose of each of us is
to mark and pass down

A bit more of the pattern of
beauty-may!

We the Lamb do what we
can do

Because we don't see the
permanence of this hell!

Perhaps, one day, other people of the heart, out of mercy, will offer an honest prayer for the Lamb!

Deep consideration in the cadence of the Seeker's Province of Flowers and refining its gates, brevity of speech was seen as proper so that upon this rich currently-sad garden and eventually-high hanged orchard, Like paradise, eight gates were placed! It became concise, so it does not lead to weariness, as today's people get bored too fast, and are distracted by many things!

The 1st Gate of Paradise: On the conduct of the anglicized

The 2nd Gate of Paradise: On the manners of the demonized

The 3rd Gate of Paradise: On the virtue of contentment

The 4th Gate of Paradise: On the benefits of being silenced

The 5th Gate of Paradise: On youth and love

The 6th Gate of Paradise: On old age and weakness

The 7th Gate of Paradise: On the effect of education

The 8th Gate: On the etiquette of companionship

And we end with the 9th Gate:
The Gate of Hell!

At our time on this planet right now, the year is 1996 after the ministry!

Our intention is advice, and we provide it!

We leave your judgment to God, and we say goodbye!